# KING SHAKA

## ZULU LEGEND

LUKE W. MOLVER

STORY PRESS AFRICA

Published by **Story Press Africa**, an imprint of
**Jive Media Africa** (South Africa) and **Catalyst Press** (USA).
**Website:** www.storypressafrica.com

**Jive Media Africa**
P O Box 22106
Mayor's Walk, 3208
South Africa

**Tel:** +27 33 342 9380/2
**Email:** admin@jivemedia.co.za
**Website:** www.jivemedia.co.za

**Catalyst Press**
2941 Kelly Street
Livermore CA 94551 USA

**Tel:** 001-925-315-5970
**Email**: jlpowers@catalystpress.org
**Website:** www.catalystpress.org

**Illustrated by:** Luke W. Molver
**Written by:** Luke W. Molver

**Acknowledgements:**  This work has drawn on
*Myth of Iron: Shaka in History* by Dan Wylie, *The Assassination of King
Shaka* by John Laband, and *Emperor Shaka the Great* by Mazisi Kunene

Fonts in the graphic text by BlamBot, used with licence.

Library of Congress Control Number:  2018967172

Trade Paper ISBN 978-1-946498-93-9
Trade Cloth ISBN 978-1-946498-90-8

FIRST EDITION

10 9 8 7 6 5 4 3 2 1

# FOREWORD

It is an honor and privilege to write the Foreword for this book, which follows on King Shaka's emergence as a leader in **Shaka Rising** and recounts the ambitions and challenges of his reign as king.

The story of the legendary King Shaka, King of the Zulu people, has fascinated ordinary people and scholars for nearly two centuries in Africa and around the world. His legacy as one of the greatest African military tacticians of the 19th century is rich with complexities, myths and ambiguities.

This book succeeds in communicating King Shaka's story because it locates him within a historical context. He was both product and shaper of the changes that were occurring in southern Africa during the late 18th and early 19th centuries. The story equips the reader with knowledge about a wide range of social and political issues including belief systems, leadership, accountability, nation-building, gender relations, diplomacy, patriotism, loyalty and strategy. This empowers the reader to comprehend the socio-economic and political developments of the early 20th century.

In addition, King Shaka's story gives the reader a better appreciation of settlement patterns in south-eastern Africa at that time, particularly in the present-day KwaZulu-Natal and Eastern Cape.

While scholars continue to debate King Shaka's role in state formation in southern Africa, there is general recognition of his role in the transformation of military strategies and the consolidation of communities in what later came to be known as Natal and Zululand. King Shaka's story is a reminder of the fluidity of ethnic and linguistic identities.

His legacy lives on – that of the distinguished leader who founded the Zulu nation – and it will continue to influence the perceptions of present and future generations.

**Dr Sibongiseni Mkhize**
Chief Executive Officer,
South African State Theatre, Pretoria

**NANDI**
("The Great She-Elephant")
King Shaka's mother and
high-ranking *inkosikazi*

**NOMCOBA**
Princess of the Zulu and
King Shaka's sister

# THE CHARACTERS IN

**KING SHAKA**
King of the Zulu and the
southern chiefdoms

**DINGANE**
Prince of the Zulu and King
Shaka's half-brother

**MHLANGANA**
Prince of the Zulu and King
Shaka's half-brother

**MNKABAYI**
("The Kingmaker") King
Shaka's aunt and high-
ranking *inkosikazi*

**NDENGEZI**
King Shaka's closest friend
and trusted advisor

**HLAMBAMANZI**
Former slave and
King Shaka's interpreter

**MANANGA**
High-ranking general in
King Shaka's army

# "KING SHAKA: ZULU LEGEND"

**NONZAMA**
Commander of the
iziYendane *ibutho*

**MAGAYE**
Chief of the Cele, allies to
the Zulu

**ZWIDE**
King of the Ndwandwe, a
northern slaver clan

**SIKHUNYANE**
Prince of the Ndwandwe
and Zwide's son and heir

**HENRY FYNN**
("Mbulazi") Port Natal settler,
hunter and mercenary

**FRANCIS
FAREWELL**
Port Natal settler, hunter

SOUTHERN AFRICA, EARLY 19TH CENTURY...

NDWANDWE
King Zwide

TO DELAGOA BAY

Pongolo River

iziYendane Raids
(1822-3)

Mkhuze River

Mzinyathi River

White Mfolozi River

Black Mfolozi River

SITHOLE

ZULU
King Shaka

Mhlatuze River

Thukela River

KwaBulawayo

INDIAN OCEAN

Mvoti River

QWABE

N

Mngeni River

CELE

W                E

Port Natal
Est. 1825

S

MPONDO

DURBAN BAY

"... IN A LAND OF KINGS..."

KING SHAKA, SINCE YOUR VICTORY AGAINST THE NDWANDWE MANY OF THE SMALLER CHIEFDOMS ARE PLEDGING THEIR SPEARS TO YOU...

... HOWEVER, IN OUR SOUTHERNMOST MARCHES, THE MPONDO CLAN REMAIN A POTENTIAL THREAT... AND IT IS SAID THEY EMPLOY DARK WITCHCRAFT TO TRANSFORM THEIR WARRIORS INTO HYENAS...

YOU FEAR FAIRYTALES, NDENGEZI? THE MPONDO WILL BE BROUGHT TO HEEL JUST LIKE THE REST.

SUCH DISTANT CHIEFDOMS ARE TOO FAR AWAY TO PRESENTLY CONCERN ME.

THE MPONDO'S OPEN RESISTANCE UNDERMINES YOUR RULE, SHAKA. THEY MUST BE MADE AN EXAMPLE OF, SO OTHER CHIEFS KNOW THEIR PLACE.

IN TIME... BUT EVERY BATTLE WE FIGHT DRAINS CRUCIAL RESOURCES.

NOW, WE MUST FOCUS ON SECURING THE LOYALTIES OF THOSE CLANS NEARER OUR BORDERS...

3

5

... BUT I ALSO NEED *MNKABAYI*.

THE *SISTER* OF *SENZANGAKHONA* IS INDEED A POWERFUL WOMAN IN THE ROYAL HOUSE. SHE *RULED* AS REGENT AFTER YOUR GRANDFATHER'S DEATH, UNTIL YOUR *FATHER* CAME OF AGE... THEY CALL HER *"THE KINGMAKER."*

BUT SHE IS ALSO RUTHLESS AND CUNNING. DO NOT FORGET THE WORDS OF HER *IZIBONGO*...

*"THE OPENER OF GATES; SO THAT PEOPLE MAY ENTER... THE SIPPER FOR OTHERS OF THE VENOM OF COBRAS."*

I HAVE NO DOUBT THAT MNKABAYI SERVES THE *KINGDOM* BEFORE THE *KING*... BUT WITHOUT HER BACKING, MY *OWN CLAIM* TO LEADERSHIP OF THE ZULU MAY NOT HAVE BEEN *SUCCESSFUL*.

YOU ARE THE ONE *TRUE* KING OF THE ZULU, MY SON. AND THIS IS THE *DAWN* OF AN AGE OF PROSPERITY FOR OUR PEOPLE.

*"AN AGE OF PROSPERITY..."* I HAVE HEARD THOSE WORDS BEFORE, MOTHER. A LONG TIME AGO, *DINGISWAYO* SPOKE THEM, AND I *BELIEVED* THEM.

HE SPOKE THE *TRUTH*. YOU HAVE ALREADY MADE THE ZULU MORE POWERFUL THAN EVER BEFORE. YOU HAVE GROWN OUR TERRITORIES *TENFOLD* BEYOND YOUR FATHER'S REIGN. BUT YOU ARE NOT JUST A *CONQUEROR*... YOU ARE A *PROTECTOR*.

YOU ARE THE *RISING SUN*... BUT YOU ARE ALSO THE *SHADE*.

REMEMBER THAT *BALANCE*, MY SON.

"WHILE THE ZULU KING STROVE TO CONSOLIDATE HIS POWER AND UNITE THE CLANS UNDER HIS RULE, THE YOUNG MESSENGER'S WARNING WAS LOST..."

"... AND FAR TO THE SOUTH, A *DANGEROUS THREAT* FROM WITHIN KING SHAKA'S OWN DOMAIN WAS SPREADING LIKE AN *INFECTED WOUND*..."

OUR TROOPS WILL REACH THE VILLAGE BY NIGHTFALL, *GENERAL NONZAMA*.

THEY WILL HAVE SEEN BY NOW THE *DUST* OF OUR *MARCHING*... THEY WILL SNATCH UP THEIR MEAGER POSSESSIONS AND ATTEMPT TO *FLEE*...

... BUT ONCE THEY GLIMPSE THE *RED* OF OUR *SHIELDS*, THEY WILL KNOW THERE IS *NO ESCAPE*.

GENERAL... BY NOW, WORD OF OUR DISLOYALTY WILL HAVE REACHED *KING SHAKA*. WE SHOULD PUSH FURTHER SOUTH, OUT OF THE REACH OF HIS—

DISLOYALTY? NO, MY FRIEND...

WE HAVE BEEN A MOST LOYAL *IBUTHO* TO THIS KING. WE HAVE EXECUTED HIS COMMANDS WITHOUT QUESTION OR *REMORSE*.

WE HAVE GONE BEYOND THE CALL OF DUTY, *SACRIFICED* MORE THAN ANY OTHERS. WITHOUT *US*, WITHOUT *THE IZIYENDANE*, HE WOULD NOT WEAR A KING'S MANTLE...

8

BUT THE KING HAS TURNED HIS BACK ON US. SO WE WILL *REMIND* HIM *WHO WE ARE.*

WHEN WE REACH THE VILLAGE, TAKE THE CATTLE. *BURN THE HOMESTEADS.*

GENERAL NONZAMA... WE HAVE RAIDED *SO MANY* VILLAGES, WE DO NOT EVEN KNOW *WHICH* CLAN LIES AHEAD...

DON'T YOU UNDERSTAND, MY FRIEND... *IT DOESN'T MATTER.*

LET A FEW OF THEM *FLEE,* TO *HERALD* OUR *MARCH.*

"THE ROGUE *IZIYENDANE IBUTHO* CONTINUED THEIR CAMPAIGN OF TERROR THROUGH THE FRINGES OF ZULU CONTROL, BUT THE KING'S FOCUS REMAINED *DISTRACTED...*"

"... CLOSER TO HOME, *SQUABBLING CHIEFS* AND *TERRITORIAL DISPUTES* SEEMED TO REQUIRE HIS CONSTANT ATTENTION."

"HOWEVER, AS IT ALWAYS IS WITH *ARROGANT MEN,* IT BECAME EASIER TO PERSUADE THE SOUTHERN CHIEFS WHEN THEY WERE GATHERED IN *CELEBRATION...* AND AS THE SPRING RAINS TURNED THE SAND TO CLAY, SO BEGAN THE *UMKHOSI* - THE *CEREMONY* OF *FIRST FRUITS.*"

"THE *ZULU* CAPITAL OF KWABULAWAYO WAS A *MAJESTIC SIGHT* TO BEHOLD..."

"LATER IN THE EVENING, AFTER THE DAY'S CELEBRATIONS HAD WANED, A *NEW VISITOR* ARRIVED BEFORE THE KING..."

ALL ARE WELCOME AT THE CEREMONY OF FIRST FRUITS, BUT YOU HAVE COME *ALONE* AND *UNKNOWN,* TRAVELER... SPEAK YOUR NAME, AND TELL ME WHAT BRINGS YOU TO THE LANDS OF THE *ZULU.*

*NKOSI SHAKA...* I AM OF THE *XHOSA* PEOPLE, TO THE WEST. I WAS A *SLAVE,* IN SERVITUDE TO THE *WHITE MEN* OF THE *CAPE COLONY...*

... I AM CALLED *HLAMBAMANZI.*

AND YOU HAVE *ESCAPED* YOUR CAPTORS TO COME TO *ME?*

*NOT EXACTLY,* KING SHAKA...

... I WAS ON A *SHIP* OF *WHITE HUNTERS.* THEY ATTEMPTED TO LAND FURTHER NORTH WHERE THE *MKUZE RIVER* MEETS THE *OCEAN...*

... BUT THEIR VESSEL WAS *WRECKED.*

I WAS *ABANDONED* ON SHORE BY THE RESCUERS... AND SO I EMBRACED MY *FREEDOM* WHILE STILL ABLE.

I COME TO PLEDGE MY ALLEGIANCE TO *YOU*, GREAT KING, WHOSE *FAME* SPREADS EVEN AS HE *SITS*...

HLAMBAMANZI... YOUR NAME MEANS *"TO SWIM THE SEAS."* PERHAPS IT IS TRUE TO YOUR NATURE, FOR THE JOURNEY HERE IS LONG AND *ARDUOUS*. BUT WHAT CAN A *LONE RABBIT* FLEEING ITS SNARE, OFFER TO A *KING*?

NKOSI... I CAN TELL YOU MUCH OF THE *WHITE SETTLERS*. I SPEAK THEIR TONGUE, AND HAVE LEARNED OF THEIR WAYS. MORE OF THEM ARRIVE EVERY YEAR, MY KING...

... AND SOONER RATHER THAN LATER, THEY *WILL* COME TO THE LANDS OF THE *ZULU*.

"KING SHAKA WELCOMED HLAMBAMANZI, FOR HE KNEW THE FUGITIVE SLAVE'S WARNING WOULD PROVE *TRUE*. BICKERING CHIEFS AND UPSTART CLANS WERE NO LONGER THE *ONLY* PROBLEMS HE FACED..."

"... *WHITE HUNTERS* AND *TRADERS* WERE ENCROACHING INTO THE SURROUNDING CHIEFDOMS, AND IT WAS ONLY A MATTER OF *TIME* BEFORE THEY ENCOUNTERED THE *ZULU*."

"NEW THREATS REQUIRED *NEW ALLIES*, AND THE MAN THEY CALLED *'SWIM-THE-SEAS'* WOULD PROVE VALUABLE TO KING SHAKA."

13

"MEANWHILE, FAR TO THE NORTH, THE *NDWANDWE* HAD RE-ESTABLISHED THEMSELVES IN THE LANDS BEYOND THE *PHONGOLO RIVER*..."

FATHER... THE RESTORATION OF OUR KINGDOM HAS BEEN DIFFICULT, BUT WE MUST SHOW THAT THE NDWANDWE ARE *STILL A POWER* TO BE *RECKONED WITH*...

YOU RATTLE BENEATH YOUR *ROYAL REGALIA*, MY SON... BUT YOU STILL DO NOT UNDERSTAND *RULERSHIP*. THERE ARE *GREATER CONCERNS* AT PLAY THAN PETTY VENGEANCE AGAINST THE *ZULU*.

RESPECTFULLY, FATHER... IT IS NOT *PETTY VENGEANCE*. THE NDWANDWE WERE NOT ONLY DEFEATED AT MHLATUZE... WE WERE *HUMILIATED*.

"WE," SIKHUNYANE? WERE *YOU* THERE, IN THE HAZE OF *HEAT* AND *SWEAT*, ASSEGAI IN HAND, *BLEEDING* IN THE *MUDDY GULCHES* OF THE *MHLATUZE?*

*NO*. YOU WERE STILL A FAT LITTLE BOY WHEN I TOOK MY ARMIES SOUTH, WHO WAILED LIKE A WOMAN WHEN YOU GRAZED A KNEE.

YOU KNOW NOTHING OF WAR, OR VENGEANCE... *<KOFF KOFF!>*

KING ZWIDE. IT IS TIME FOR ME TO ADMINISTER THE *UMUTHI*.

FATHER, YOUR *ILLNESS* CONTINUES *UNABATED*. THESE HERBS AND POULTICES DO NOTHING BUT *BEFOUL* THE HUT WITH THEIR *STENCH*...

YOU SHOULD NOT *CONCERN* YOURSELF WITH MATTERS BEYOND YOUR *COMPREHENSION*, PRINCE SIKHUNYANE.

*QUIET*, BOTH OF YOU. INYANGA, PREPARE MY MEDICINES.

SIKHUNYANE... *LEAVE US*.

WHEN THE NDWANDWE DESCENDED ON OUR LANDS, THEY RAZED MY HOMESTEAD, BURNED MY FIELDS. THEY DID NOT TAKE CROPS, OR EVEN LIVESTOCK...

... ONLY *PEOPLE.*

MEN, WOMEN AND *CHILDREN.* THOSE THAT WERE TOO OLD OR TOO YOUNG OR TOO SICKLY, THEY *KILLED.* THEY *PUT FIRE* TO EVERYTHING ELSE.

I *FLED,* WITH AS MANY OTHERS AS WERE ABLE. WE BECAME CRIMINALS OURSELVES, REFUGEE RAIDERS FORCED TO PLUNDER AND SCAVENGE FOR *SURVIVAL,* BEFORE THE EVER-EXPANDING RIPPLE OF *SLAVERY.*

WHEN WE PLEDGED OUR SPEARS TO YOU, IT WAS BECAUSE WE *BELIEVED* IN YOU. THAT YOU WOULD GIVE US BACK SOME DIGNITY, SOME SEMBLANCE OF HONOR AS WARRIORS...

... WE SHED OUR BLOOD AT THE BATTLE OF THE MHLATUZE...

... WE *DIED* FOR YOU.

BUT YOU LET THE NDWANDWE *RETREAT.* YOU ALLOWED THEM TO FLEE, WHEN YOU COULD HAVE *CRUSHED THEM.* YOU DISHONORED YOUR OWN WARRIORS WITH YOUR *"MERCY"* TO OUR ENEMIES...

YOU MURDERED *WOMEN* AND *CHILDREN.*

WE TOOK WHAT WE WERE *OWED.* AFTER THE BATTLE OF MHLATUZE, YOU SENT US TO THE *ARMPIT* OF THE SOUTHERN MARCHES TO COLLECT *DUNG-WORTHY TRIBUTES* FROM *WAYWARD CHIEFLINGS.* YOU *FORGOT* THOSE WITH *NOTHING,* WHO HAD ONLY THEIR SPEARS AND THEIR LIVES TO PLEDGE TO YOU...

... YOU FORGOT *US,* AS YOU PLAYED YOUR *KINGLY GAMES* WITH ALL YOUR NEW *"ALLIES."*

BUT YOU WILL REMEMBER THE IZIYENDANE *NOW,* KING SHAKA.

YOU WILL BE REMEMBERED AS *BUTCHERS.* YOUR LANDS WILL BE TAKEN, AND YOUR CATTLE GIVEN TO THE SURVIVORS OF YOUR MASSACRES. NO IMPHEPHO WILL BE BURNT FOR YOU, AND NO IZIBONGO SUNG.

YOUR NAMES WILL BE CAST TO THE WINDS, NEVER TO BE SPOKEN AGAIN.

BUT KNOW THIS, NONZAMA... THE *NDWANDWE* WILL YET *PAY* FOR THEIR ACTIONS...

... AS MUST YOU.

SSHLUKKT!

"MEANWHILE, FURTHER SOUTH, ANOTHER OF KING SHAKA'S AMABUTHO HAD STUMBLED ON AN *UNUSUAL SIGHT* WHILE RETURNING FROM A CAMPAIGN..."

GENERAL MANANGA... WHAT... ARE WE *LOOKING AT?*

WHITE PEOPLE.

AND THE STORIES I HAVE HEARD OF THEM ARE *NOT FAVORABLE*... THIS CLOSE TO OUR LANDS, KING SHAKA MUST BE INFORMED.

MOBILIZE OUR FORCES. WE SHALL GREET THESE *VISITORS*, AND ACCOMPANY THEM TO THE KING, AS GUESTS OF THE ZULU...

"AND THUS DID THE ZULU ENCOUNTER THE WHITE MEN FOR THE *FIRST TIME*, STRUGGLING AND SHOUTING AND *DROWNING* AMIDST THE *SPLINTERED WRECKAGE* OF THEIR VESSEL, UNCEREMONIOUSLY MAROONED ON A *FOREIGN SHORE*..."

"WITH ASSISTANCE FROM THE ZULU IBUTHO, THE SHIPWRECK SURVIVORS WERE RESCUED FROM THEIR ORDEAL, AND ESCORTED TO *KWABULAWAYO*. THE WHITE MEN WERE NOT PRISONERS, AND WERE PERMITTED TO RETAIN THEIR SUPPLIES AND *FOREIGN WEAPONS...*"

"... HOWEVER, WITH NO SHARED LANGUAGE TO *COMMUNICATE*, MANY WERE *FEARFUL*... SOME WERE *CURIOUS*..."

"... AND SOME OF THE PALE FACES EVEN LOOKED STRANGELY *PLEASED* AT THIS TURN OF EVENTS, WHICH PUT THEIR *FATES* IN THE HANDS OF THE *ZULU*."

"A *GREAT CROWD* GATHERED AT KWABULAWAYO TO RECEIVE THE VISITORS, INCLUDING CHIEFS FROM OTHER CLANS... MANY WERE CURIOUS ABOUT THE *STRANGE NEWCOMERS*, WHO HAD ARRIVED LIKE *SWALLOWS* FROM ACROSS THE SEA."

25

"AS KING SHAKA FOSTERED NEW ALLIANCES, THE *AMAKHOSIKAZI* DISCUSSED MATTERS OF THEIR KINGDOM, AND THEIR *KING...*"

KING SHAKA HAS WELCOMED THESE *WHITE SWALLOWS* INTO OUR LANDS, AND ALLOWS THEM TO *NEST...*

... BUT HE TREATS THEM LIKE *PETS,* AND UNDERESTIMATES THEIR *DUPLICITY!*

OUR KING TREATS THEM LIKE *ASSETS,* TO SERVE THE PURPOSES OF THE *ZULU.* TRIBUTE WILL BE EXACTED FROM THE NEW *WHITE AMAKHANDA* JUST LIKE IT IS EVERYWHERE ELSE.

YES, TRIBUTE WILL BE EXACTED... BUT IT WILL *NOT* BE LIKE ANYWHERE ELSE. THE WHITES OFFER *UNIQUE* BENEFITS, AND *DANGERS...* AND THE LANDS PLUNDERED BY THE IZIYENDANE LEAVE *MUCH ROOM* FOR THEM TO *SPREAD.*

MY BROTHER WILL NOT ALLOW THESE *IVORY-HUNGRY* WHITE HUNTERS FREE REIGN OF OUR LANDS. OUR KING WOULD ENTER NO ALLIANCE THAT WOULD *JEOPARDIZE* THE ZULU *HOMELANDS...*

... BUT HE SEES THE *USES* OF THE SWALLOWS. THEIR *GUNS.* THEIR *MEDICINES...*

*TOYS* AND *OINTMENTS,* NOMCOBA. THE SWALLOWS BRING *MUCH MORE.* NEW OPPORTUNITIES. TRADE ROUTES. BUSINESS PARTNERSHIPS. THEY OFFER AN *ALTERNATIVE FUTURE* FOR THE ZULU...

"... A FUTURE THAT KING SHAKA MUST CONSIDER *VERY CAREFULLY.*"

"AND SO, WITH THE CONSIDERABLE AID OF THE ZULU, THE WHITE SETTLEMENT OF *PORT NATAL* WAS ESTABLISHED AT THE HARBOR OF *ISIBUBULUNGU...*"

"KING SHAKA RECEIVED HIS *TRIBUTES* FROM THE *NEW SETTLERS* ON HIS SHORES... "

"... BUT *BRITTLE* IS THE BRANCH OF *LOYALTY,* WHEN WEIGHED DOWN BY THE *AMBITIONS* OF *AVARICIOUS MEN.*"

"THE SEASONS CYCLED AND THE *FIRST FRUITS CEREMONY* DAWNED ONCE MORE. IT WAS THE FIRST SINCE THE ARRIVAL OF THE *WHITE MEN,* AND KING SHAKA INVITED THE NEW SETTLERS TO ATTEND THE CELEBRATIONS AT KWABULAWAYO..."

YOUR FRIEND *MISTER FAREWELL* HAS DECLINED MY INVITATION, IT WOULD SEEM...

34

39

SOME TIME LATER, BEYOND THE PHONGOLO RIVER, IN THE NDWANDWE LANDS...

THE *ANCESTORS* HAVE CALLED OUT FOR YOUR *FATHER*...

... AND HE HAS *ANSWERED THEM.*

*YOU* ARE NOW *KING* OF THE *NDWANDWE,* SIKHUNYANE.

MY FATHER... GREW *WEAK* FROM HIS *SICKNESS.* IT *DECAYED* HIS BODY AND TURNED HIS MIND *SOFT* AS IMPHEPHO SMOKE...

"... LIKE THE *CRASHING* OF A *THOUSAND WAVES*..."

*I* WILL RETURN OUR PEOPLE TO THEIR FORMER *GLORY,* AND REGAIN OUR *HONOR*... I WILL BRING THE NDWANDWE ARMIES DOWN UPON THE ZULU ONCE MORE...

KING SHAKA...

"PEACE..."

"... AN *ASSASSIN'S SPEAR* WAS A SHARP REMINDER THAT IT TORE APART JUST AS EASILY AS *FLESH.*"

"AS THE ZULU MARCHED TOWARD THEIR FINAL BATTLE WITH THE NDWANDWE, THE WORDS OF THE TRAITOR *NONZAMA* ECHOED IN KING SHAKA'S EARS..."

... "THE CENTER CANNOT HOLD..."

THE ZULU HOMELANDS.

I REMEMBER A TIME FROM YOUR CHILDHOOD, *PRINCE DINGANE*...

... YOUR BROTHER *SIGUJANA* WAS *BEATING* YOU FOR PLAYING WITH HIS *TOY.* YOU WERE SMALLER AND WEAKER, AND HE TOOK PLEASURE IN YOUR *TORMENT*...

... UNTIL *SHAKA'S FIST* BROKE HIS NOSE, AND LEFT HIM *BAWLING* ON THE GROUND LIKE AN *INFANT.*

BOTH *YOU* AND *SHAKA* WERE SEVERELY *PUNISHED* BY *SENZANGAKHONA*, FOR INJURING HIS *FAVORITE* SON... BUT SIGUJANA NEVER AGAIN *TORMENTED* YOU WHEN SHAKA WAS NEARBY.

SO WHY, PRINCE OF THE ZULU, WOULD YOU WISH THE *DOWNFALL* OF THE BROTHER WHO PROTECTED YOU SO MANY TIMES?

YOU REMEMBER MUCH, WISE MNKABAYI... IT IS WHY I SEEK YOUR *COUNSEL.*

KING SHAKA HAS BECOME *RECKLESS.* EVEN NOW, HE MARCHES OUR ARMIES NORTH TO ENGAGE THE NDWANDWE, WHILE HE SHOULD BE AT HIS IKHANDA, DELEGATING HIS GENERALS IN SUCH WAR EFFORTS... THE KING *ABANDONS* HIS PEOPLE TO ENDANGER *HIMSELF.*

THE ZULU NEED MORE *STABLE* HANDS TO MOLD THEIR FUTURE...

... *YOUR HANDS,* DINGANE?

WE ARE AN *AGRICULTURAL PEOPLE.* OUR KING IS NO HOT-HEADED *WARMONGER.* IN HIS RAIDS, HIS CAMPAIGNS... KING SHAKA SEEKS *RESOURCES* FOR OUR NATION. NOT ONLY TO SURVIVE, BUT TO *THRIVE...*

... BEYOND EVEN THE TIME WHEN HE HIMSELF WILL BE *ASH* AND *DUST.*

MNKABAYI... HE IS FILLED WITH *DOUBT* THESE PAST MONTHS. SINCE THE ATTEMPT ON HIS *LIFE...*

YES... *ODD,* HOW THE ASSASSIN WAS NEVER *FOUND.* THE COURT OF KING SHAKA IS INDEED *SHROUDED* IN SHADOWS.

BUT DO NOT FORGET, DINGANE... I AM THE *KINGMAKER.* I HAVE WITNESSED THE ZULU CYCLE THROUGH GENERATIONS OF RULERS, LIKE SUNRISE AND SUNSET...

... AND IN MY EXPERIENCE, FEW THINGS DISTINGUISH ONE *BELLIGERENT CHIEF* FROM THE *NEXT.*

THAT IS WHY TRUE RULERSHIP IS MEASURED NOT IN *CONQUEST...*

... BUT IN *SACRIFICE.*

WHAT HAVE *YOU* SACRIFICED, DINGANE?

THE *IZINDOLOWANE HILLS*, NEAR THE *PHONGOLO RIVER*...

YOU SWALLOWS MAY HAVE SOME *STRANGE* IDEAS...

... BUT YOUR TOOLS ARE OF *CUNNING CONSTRUCTION*.

NKOSI... OUR AMABUTHO HAVE *SURROUNDED* THE VALLEY.

SIKHUNYANE IS ENCAMPED WITH THE MAIN NDWANDWE ARMY IN THE FOREST, WHILE THEIR WOMEN AND CHILDREN ARE A SHORT DISTANCE UP THE RIVER. BEYOND THAT, A SMALLER CONTINGENT OF THEIR FORCES GUARDS THE CATTLE.

THEY CELEBRATE THEIR RECENT RAIDS WITH *BEER* AND *REVELRY*, OBLIVIOUS TO OUR PRESENCE.

WE WILL ALLOW THEM THEIR *SLUMBER* TONIGHT... AND WHEN THE SUN'S FIRST RAYS BREAK ACROSS THE VALLEY, WE WILL *STRIKE*.

MHLANGANA, NDENGEZI - YOU WILL TAKE THE AMABUTHO INTO THE FOREST AND SHAKE THE NDWANDWE AWAKE WITH *SPEAR* AND *FIRE*. THOSE THAT BREAK THE TREELINE WILL BE *SHOT DOWN* BY MBULAZI AND HIS GUNMEN....

MANANGA, YOUR AMABUTHO WILL CLOSE IN FROM HERE, SCATTERING THEIR CATTLE TO THROW THEIR ESCAPE INTO *CHAOS*.

45

"OLD ENEMIES WERE DEFEATED ON THAT BURNING DAWN... BUT NEW TREACHERY WAS MASKED IN THE BLOODSHED OF BATTLE."

"BACK IN THE LANDS OF THE SOUTH, THE WHITE SETTLEMENT OF PORT NATAL HAD BECOME A HAVEN FOR *FUGITIVES* AND *CRIMINALS.* *FRANCIS FAREWELL* HAD *EXPANDED* WHITE TERRITORY, OCCUPYING AREAS PREVIOUSLY RAVAGED BY THE *IZIYENDANE.*"

"MOREOVER, A CRIPPLING *DROUGHT* HAD TAKEN HOLD OF THE KINGDOM..."

"THE FIRST RAINS HAD BEEN LITTLE MORE THAN A SMATTERING OF *DROPLETS,* AND THE TRADITIONAL *RITUALS* TO APPEASE THE ANCESTORS HAD NOT BEEN *ANSWERED...*"

"... BUT IT WAS A FAR MORE PERSONAL MELANCHOLY THAT WEIGHED ON THE KING AFTER HIS RETURN..."

NOMCOBA.

*NDENGEZI* IS WITH THE *ANCESTORS.*

HE FOUGHT *BRAVELY,* AND DIED WITH HONOR. A *WARRIOR'S DEATH.*

A WARRIOR'S *PLATITUDES,* THAT YOU CAN SAVE FOR HIS *PRAISES...*

... HE LOVED YOU AS A *BROTHER.*

Central Islip Public Library
33 Hawthorne Avenue
Central Islip, NY 11722

I AM *FILLED* WITH *DOUBTS,* MOTHER... THE *ANCESTORS* CALL OUT FOR YOU, BUT THE *ZULU* STILL NEED YOUR GENTLE *WISDOM...*

I AM *PREPARED* FOR THIS JOURNEY, MY SON... BUT THE *CROWN* OF THE *ZULU* IS A HEAVY HEAD-DRESS TO WEAR, AND KINGS HAVE OFTEN BEEN *BLINKERED* BY ITS GRANDIOSE BEADS AND FEATHERS.

A *WISE RULER* CASTS HIS GAZE ALL AROUND HIMSELF, FROM *YESTERDAY'S SUNSET* TO THE *DAWN* OF *TOMORROW.*

A WISE RULER LEARNS THE *LESSONS* OF THE ANCESTORS, AND PREPARES HIS PEOPLE FOR A *FUTURE* BEYOND HIS OWN RULE.

A WISE RULER IS NOT A SPEAR... BUT A *SHIELD.*

"AND SO DID THE *GREAT SHE-ELEPHANT,* THE *QUEEN REGENT* OF THE *ZULU,* DEPART THIS WORLD FOR THE *AFTERLIFE...*"

"IN THE ARMS OF HER *SON,* BENEATH THE *STARS* OF HER *PEOPLE.*"

"*BELOVED* BY THE PEOPLE AS BOTH *WISE* AND *JUST*, NANDI'S PASSING WRACKED THE ZULU KINGDOM WITH *MOURNING*..."

"... AND DEEPENED THE *DARK TIDES* THAT CRASHED INSIDE KING SHAKA'S HEART."

"ACROSS THE KINGDOM, HUNDREDS OF CATTLE WERE *SACRIFICED*, AND A THOUSAND SONGS WERE *SUNG*... RAIDS FOR GRAIN AND LIVESTOCK BECAME *MASSIVE CAMPAIGNS* IN NANDI'S HONOR..."

"... WHILE EVEN IN THE MIDST OF A *NATION'S MOURNING*, FORCES STILL *CONSPIRED* TO BEND RUMOR AND HEARSAY AGAINST THE KING."

"IN THAT TIME OF SORROW, ONLY *TEARS* FELL UPON THE *THIRSTY EARTH*."

"KING SHAKA'S SHADOW FELL LONG ACROSS THE LAND, BUT WITHIN THAT SHADE, SPEARS WERE BEING SHARPENED..."

MNKABAYI. SINCE THE BATTLE AGAINST THE *NDWANDWE*, A SHROUD HAS COVERED THE *KING*... AND HIS MOTHER'S *DEATH* HAS SENT HIM TUMBLING YET *FURTHER* INTO DARKNESS.

THE EVENTS AT THE IZINDOLOWANE HILLS SHOW HIS BEHAVIOR HAS BECOME *VIOLENT* AND *UNPREDICTABLE*. HE SPENDS HIS DAYS BROODING AND *STARING* AT THE *SEA*, AND GIVES AWAY EVER MORE TO THE *SWALLOWS*...

... EVEN NOW, A *DELEGATION* TRAVELS TO THE CAPE TO *FAWN* AT THE FEET OF THE *WHITE LEADERS*.

DINGANE...

YES, *NDLOVUKAZI*?

... PUT MORE *WOOD* ON THE *FIRE*.

MNKABAYI... YOU ARE NOW THE GREAT *SHE-ELEPHANT*...

... YOUR BACKING WILL GIVE *SUPPORT* TO *MY* CLAIM...

... I *MUST* BE THE NEW *KING* OF THE *ZULU*.

64

65

66

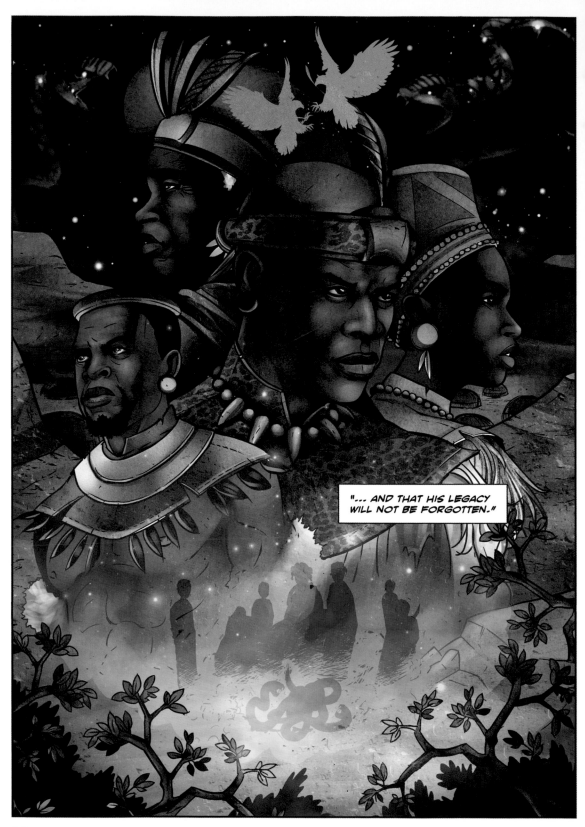

# THE STORY CONTINUES

During his reign, King Shaka established the Zulu people as the dominant power among the peoples of south-eastern Africa. After his death, many of his highly effective tactics were continued by his brother King Dingane and his successors. This made the Zulu a formidable force for the next fifty years, and a significant challenge to white settlers and British colonial ambitions.

When Dingane became king, he purged further threats to his rule. The executions included his brother and co-conspirator Mhlangana, proving King Shaka's alleged final words to be hauntingly prophetic.

The expansion of British control and Boer settlements gave rise to ongoing tension between the Zulu and the white newcomers, culminating in the Anglo-Zulu War, fought in 1879. The Zulu military tactics perfected by Shaka led to a humiliating rout of the British army at Isandlwana. Yet later in that year British firepower finally defeated King Cetshwayo's armies at Ulundi.

O MY BROTHERS, YOU WOULD BE *KINGS* OF THE *EARTH*...

... BUT BEWARE YOUR *BARGAINS* WITH THE *SWALLOWS*, FOR THEIR WINGS WILL BLOCK THE SUN FROM OUR KINGDOM...

SEE PAGE 66

King Shaka's legacy lives on. He established a succession of Zulu kings which continues to this day. The current monarch is King Goodwill Zwelithini and the Zulu people number some 12 million – almost a quarter of South Africa's population – and they regard King Shaka as the founder of their nation.

# HOW ACCURATE IS THIS STORY ?

*King Shaka* is a "historical fiction" based, as far as possible, on fact. But there are different versions of his story, and this is merely one "telling" of the story. Zulu culture had no written records at that time. It was an oral culture which transmitted its history through the telling and retelling of stories. It was only when Europeans arrived that details of Zulu culture were written down for the first time. These written records were produced mostly by European writers with their own very different "outsider" perspectives.

Oral history can be unreliable. As stories were passed down from each generation to the next, story tellers might exaggerate, select or embellish details. They might want to impress their listeners or portray a character's actions in a favorable light. The accuracy of their memories would differ. All these could lead to very different versions.

WILL YOU TELL US A *STORY* TONIGHT, GOGO...?

SEE PAGE 1

Written records can be just as unreliable. In most cases the writers would not have spoken the local language, did not understand the customs of the people they were writing about, and had very different ideas of land ownership and property rights. Most of the documentary records of King Shaka's time were authored by Europeans. In the past, they have been treated as historical fact. More recent research has revealed the ignorance or bias of the writers.

The diary of the Englishman Henry Francis Fynn is an example. His journal is one of the more comprehensive written records relaying events and information about the Zulu kingdom in the 1820s and 1830s. Nonetheless, it is riddled with contradictions, exaggerations and even outright lies. This served the purpose of painting a picture of Fynn, Farewell and the other early white British settlers as explorers and pioneers. In reality, they were primarily traders and hunters with commercial obligations to merchants in the Cape, although they tried to avoid British trading regulations.

SEE PAGE 32

HE IS A *STRANGE* MAN, PREOCCUPIED WITH HIS SCRAPS OF PAPER AND THEIR *SCRIBBLED SYMBOLS.* HE PERSISTS IN ASKING ME TO PUT MY *MARK* UPON THEM... BELIEVING THIS SOMEHOW BESTOWS A *KING'S AUTHORITY.*

They did their best to maintain good relations with King Shaka, and this meant serving him like subordinate chiefs, which included military obligations. Other writings from white settlers must also be read with a discerning eye, as they were recorded by people who had their own agendas.

What really happened is, therefore, often difficult to prove. The best we can do is look at all available records and come to our own conclusions about the most convincing version of the truth.

For some aspects of King Shaka's life there are very few records or none at all. In *King Shaka* some elements of the story have been fabricated for the sake of exploring "what might have been." For example, the character of Nonzama, commander of the rogue iziYendane ibutho, was based on a real person. However, little is known of the reasons for his treachery. These reasons are imagined in the comic as a catalyst for King Shaka's own self-doubt and to dramatize the dilemmas of rulership.

# THE HISTORICAL SETTING OF KING SHAKA'S TIME

The events of *King Shaka* take place in the 1820s, soon after the story of *Shaka Rising*, and trace approximately the final eight years of the Zulu king's life.

Unreliable records notwithstanding, it seems that King Shaka was probably born in the early 1780s. To give some global context to his life, he was born shortly after America had gained independence from British Rule (1776), and before the French Revolution (1789).

When he was born, the Zulu were a small clan living approximately 200 kilometers (125 miles) north-east of the present-day port of Durban. After becoming king, he quickly elevated the Zulu to their position as one of the most dominant clans of southern Africa. He was the first Zulu leader to deal with European colonization and white settlement encroaching on his lands.

The timeline shows the succession of the three Zulu kings who held power after King Shaka's death, and the important historical events that punctuated their reigns.

**KEY EVENTS IN ZULU HISTORY 1828–1879**

Death of King Shaka

Dingane executes Boer delegation

**1828** — King Dingane kaSenzangakhona, ruled 1828–1840

**1837** — Boers invade the Zulu kingdom

**1838** — Boers defeat Zulu forces at Ncome

**1839**

**1840** — Boer republic of Natalia established south of Thukela River

SEE PAGE 23

Fynn and Farewell were among the first white arrivals to venture on to Zulu soil; but they were not the last. King Shaka's first embassies to the Cape Colony aimed to obtain military intelligence, but were also genuine attempts to open official relations between the Zulu and the British. Unfortunately, these efforts were consistently undermined by greed, misconceptions, treachery and fear on both sides.

After King Shaka's death, his successor King Dingane fared no better in creating relations with the British. By this

British annexation of Boer republics and Port Natal

Death of King Mpande

British invade the Zulu kingdom

**1840**

**1856**

**1872**

**1879**

**1879**

King Mpande kaSenzangakhona, ruled 1840-1872

Natal established as separate British colony

King Cetshwayo kaMpande, ruled 1872–1879

Zulu victory at battle of Isandlwana

Decisive British victory at battle of Ulundi, Cetshwayo deposed

"AND SO, WITH THE CONSIDERABLE AID OF THE ZULU, THE WHITE SETTLEMENT OF *PORT NATAL* WAS ESTABLISHED AT THE HARBOR OF *ISIBUBULUNGU...*"

"KING SHAKA RECEIVED HIS *TRIBUTES* FROM THE *NEW SETTLERS* ON HIS SHORES... "

SEE PAGE 31

time, the Zulu were also increasingly coming into conflict with the Boers, Dutch settlers who had left the Cape Colony in the mid-1830s and sought to establish new republics of their own – one of which, the Republic of Natalia, occupied some Zulu territory. These conflicts escalated when King Dingane had an entire Boer delegation put to death, sparking a series of bloody battles between the Zulu and the Boers, culminating in The Battle of Ncome (popularly known as the "Battle of Blood River"). King Dingane's forces suffered a heavy defeat in this clash, and Dingane ceded the Boers all Zulu territory south of the Thukela River.

Soon afterwards his brother Mpande forged an alliance with the Boers. This enabled Mpande to overthrow King Dingane and become king himself. In 1843 the British annexed the Boer Republic of Natalia (including the land Dingane had ceded the Boers) as the colony of Natal and recognized the Zulu kingdom north of the Thukela.

This rising tide of white colonization displaced many thousands and led to much bloody conflict over the next decades. The independence of the Zulu kingdom finally came to an end in 1879, when British forces invaded KwaZulu (Zululand) and defeated the Zulu under King Cetshwayo. But this was only after the Zulu army had inflicted a humiliating defeat on the British at Isandlwana – the worst defeat ever suffered by a British force at the hands of an indigenous people defending their territory.

SEE
PAGE
57

... YOU SEE THROUGH THEIR *DECEPTIONS*. MISTER *FAREWELL* HAS CONTINUOUSLY SHOWN HIMSELF TO BE DRIVEN BY A RAVENING *LUST* FOR LAND AND IVORY...

# THE CHALLENGES OF LEADERSHIP

In 1824 the Zulu encountered white people for the first time when Henry Fynn and company were shipwrecked on the cost near isiBubulungu, later known as Port Natal, where they intended to settle and trade. The whites were woefully under-prepared to survive on this unknown coast, and would have perished without the considerable aid of the Zulu. Although King Shaka was wary of the new arrivals, he provided timber and a workforce to help build the settlement that would become Port Natal.

At different stages during his reign King Shaka had many different leadership roles to play. During the events of *King Shaka* he united local chiefdoms, led his people into battle,

SEE PAGE 46

NO PRISONERS WILL BE TAKEN.

helped establish the white settlers at Port Natal in exchange for tributes of ivory and firepower, and ultimately sent a Zulu embassy to the Cape Colony in an attempt to open dialogue with the British.

King Shaka had to keep these roles and many more in a delicate balance with each other – a balance that was often very difficult to maintain. King Shaka's people wanted safety and prosperity. His brothers plotted for power. The Ndwandwe sought slaves and revenge. The British hunter-traders wanted access to ivory and a secure settlement. The Boers wanted to establish their own little republic on Zulu soil. Inside and outside the Zulu kingdom, turbulent change was taking place, and King Shaka had to prioritize where to focus his energies and resources. To protect his people's future he needed to adapt to a shifting socio-political landscape that no Zulu leader had faced before.

These issues, and the ways in which King Shaka chose to manage them, created an unavoidable separation between the king and his people. Those friends and family closest

## KEY EVENTS DURING KING SHAKA'S REIGN

**1819** Shaka defeats the Ndwandwe at the Mhlatuze River

**1820** New Zulu capital is established at KwaBulawayo

**1821**

**1822**

**1823** Renegade iziYendane *ibutho* ravages the southern reaches of Shaka's kingdom to him – Nomcoba, Nandi and Ndengezi – were ultimately distanced, making King Shaka a legendary figure, but also a lonely one.

King Shaka upset much of the status quo for his people with his methods of rule, and this did not please everybody. However, it is undeniable that his reign laid the groundwork for the kings who followed him, and his legacy lives on even today.

SEE PAGE 57

| **1824** | **1825** | **1826** | **1827** | **1828** |
|---|---|---|---|---|
| Henry Fynn and company are shipwrecked on the coast near the Zulu homelands | With Zulu aid, the white settlement of Port Natal is established at isiBubulungu | The Ndwandwe are decisively defeated by the Zulu at the izinDolowane hills | Nandi dies, and Shaka sends his first embassy to the Cape Colony | Death of King Shaka |

# ZULU POLITICAL STRUCTURES

King Shaka's rise to power and period of rule can be seen as a departure from the existing system of localized chiefdoms – each consisting of a cluster of homesteads which housed extended family groups – in favor of a more complex state. When he took leadership of the Zulu, King Shaka united many of the disparate chiefdoms into one organized kingdom under his rule. He was able to command and extract labor from these allied chiefdoms both for military service and for building projects. In return he offered protection, helped resolve disputes, and allowed the various chiefs conditional autonomy over their own lands. King Shaka's rule was an elaborate but effective balance of social, political, and economic obligations, backed by military power.

SEE PAGE 11

"THE ZULU RULER HAD QUICKLY REALIZED THAT EVEN DURING TIMES OF CELEBRATION, THAT DANCE OF POLITICS NEVER ENDED... AND *PETTY RIVALRIES* AND *SIMMERING DISCONTENT* COULD BRING AN *EMPIRE* TO ITS *KNEES.*"

SEE PAGE 8

An important aspect of King Shaka's success in building the Zulu kingdom was his extensive use of the *amabutho* (singular: *ibutho*). Roughly translated as "regiments," these were more akin to mobile, multi-purpose labor forces that could number anywhere between a few hundred and several thousand men. Their numerous roles included raiding other chiefdoms or exacting tribute from them, establishing new *amakhanda* (royal military homesteads) and enforcing King Shaka's rule in outlying areas. Each *ibutho* had its own name and distinguished itself with specific colors and regalia. The iziYendane, for example, were known for their red shields and dreadlocked hair.

# THE ROLE OF WOMEN

Zulu society in King Shaka's time was patriarchal, like most societies throughout history, and many still today. Men held power and authority over women, children and lesser-ranked men. A man was the head of his household. Yet women had a crucial part to play, and could be very influential in the politics of Zulu society.

The day-to-day roles of women included running the household, growing the crops, and raising the children. Typically this was done communally by all the women of a homestead. Women were also used as political devices: through marriage, clans could strengthen relations and form new alliances.

In *King Shaka*, we also see the key role played by the *amakhosikazi*, or female elders. High-ranking women in the

KING SHAKA HAS WELCOMED THESE **WHITE SWALLOWS** INTO OUR LANDS, AND ALLOWS THEM TO **NEST**...

SEE PAGE 27

royal house, such as King Shaka's mother Nandi and his aunt Mnkabayi, held considerable influence in society, and were often consulted for advice or guidance. Mnkabayi herself was known as "The Kingmaker," reputed by many accounts to have been instrumental in the succession of Senzangakhona, Shaka and Dingane to their positions as kings of the Zulu.

POWERFUL CHIEFS ARE TOO OFTEN *ARROGANT MEN,* SHAKA... AND *AMBITION* IS A *POTENT* DRIVE.

SEE PAGE 6

The role of the *amakhosikazi* also included overseeing marriage alliances, directing distribution of provisions and managing the products of the women's agricultural labor.

King Shaka's appointment of the *amakhosikazi* to his outlying royal homesteads (*amakhanda*) is an example of the king's unique shrewdness. While their presence as King Shaka's proxies would offset the ambitions of potentially troublesome chiefs, they could never, as women, be a direct genealogical threat.

Perhaps of understated importance was the role of elder women (such as Gogo) as storytellers. More than simple night-time tales for the children, these oral storytelling traditions formed an important generational history of the Zulu people at the time, a tradition that continues today.

SEE PAGE 43

BUT DO NOT FORGET, DINGANE... I AM THE *KINGMAKER.*

SEE PAGE 52

I WILL KILL NO MORE BROTHERS!

# SIBLINGS

In this story we encounter King Shaka's sister Nomcoba, and his half-brothers Dingane, Mhlangana, and briefly, Sigujana. They shared a father but had different mothers.

If you have any siblings, you will likely be familiar with the close bonds that you form, as well as the rivalries that occur. The same was true of Shaka, Dingane, Mhlangana and Sigujana as they grew up together. Despite these bonds, there came a time when the brothers would kill each other to eliminate rivals and become king.

Compare this with the relationship King Shaka had with Nomcoba. The two trusted and cared for each other, and she saw King Shaka's reluctance to kill another brother – even though King Shaka probably suspected Dingane of conspiring against him.

# THE ROYAL HOMESTEAD

The Zulu capital of KwaBulawayo, arguably King Shaka's most famous homestead (*ikhanda*), was situated some twenty kilometers (12½ miles) north-east of present-day Eshowe. While Henry Fynn's exaggerated records attest that it was between two and three miles in circumference, the reality is probably closer to about 350 meters (1150 feet) from the lowest gate to the royal enclosure, or *isigodlo*, at the top.

The *isigodlo* was the most tightly guarded area of a large Zulu homestead, furthest from the main gate. This is where the king would stay. The other inhabitants of the *isigodlo* were elderly female relations or widows of his predecessor, the king's wives (if he had any), maidens given in tribute to serve as the king's concubines and to marry out in return for a bride-price (*ilobolo*), and female servants, often captured in war.

SEE PAGE 24

Certain ceremonies would also take place within this royal enclosure. The operations of the *isigodlo* and its women were typically the responsibility of the *amakhosikazi*.

# ZULU CULTURE AND BELIEFS

In Zulu culture, belief in the supernatural was an important aspect of their understanding of life and death. The spirits of the ancestors (*amadlozi*) were believed to influence health and human relations – for good or for bad.

Herbalists, known as *izinyanga*, could diagnose and treat physical ailments using medicines prepared from various plants. *Izangoma* were diviners believed to have direct contact with the *amadlozi* (ancestors) from whom they sought help to discern the future, grant favorable conditions, wish ill upon another person, and solve or create conflict within relationships. They also used medicines (*imithi*) in their treatments, prepared from plants and animal parts.

In the Zulu belief system, the realms of the living and the dead were inextricably linked. The *amadlozi* watched and communicated through signs and symbolism. Snakes in particular were a common vessel for *amadlozi* who wished to revisit the world of the living.

SEE PAGE 2

Ritual and ceremony were important parts of Zulu culture, and the *umKhosi*, or First Fruits Ceremony, was the grandest example of this. The umKhosi was typically an exuberant and impressive display of rain-dancing, ritual medicines, prayers to the ancestors, and cattle sacrifices to honor them. The king, as the great rain-maker, was ritually "strengthened" against his enemies and the allegiance of his subjects was reaffirmed.

# Language and naming

The Zulu language, *isiZulu*, makes use of many idioms and metaphors. For example, instead of King Shaka saying, "You have stabbed me," he says to his brothers: "You have reddened your spears in my flesh."

Another example is the metaphor used to refer to the white settlers as swallows. Ndengezi asks King Shaka: "Is it wise to allow the white swallows to fly so freely?"

A popular custom was that of praise poetry, or *izibongo*, which made extensive use of idioms. The praise poet (*imbongi*) would sing the praises of a particular chief or warrior as a form of entertainment, as well as a chronicle of the person's deeds. Often praises were also co-opted from conquered chiefs and added to those of the victor.

King Shaka's praises were numerous and elaborate, often recognizing his royal lineage and exalting his heroic military prowess:

*"He who beats but is not beaten*
*The voracious one of Senzangakhona*
*Whose  spear is red, even on the handle."*

*"He whose fame spreads*
*Even as he sits."*

Even some of the white settlers began to amass their own *izibongo*, as they became increasingly involved in Zulu campaigns. The lines below are from the praises of Henry Fynn, and describe specific aspects of the man himself:

YOU ARE THE **RISING SUN...** BUT YOU ARE ALSO THE **SHADE.**

SEE PAGE 7

SEE PAGE 13

HLAMBAMANZI... YOUR NAME MEANS "TO SWIM THE SEAS." PERHAPS IT IS TRUE TO YOUR NATURE, FOR THE JOURNEY HERE IS LONG AND ARDUOUS. BUT WHAT CAN A LONE RABBIT FLEEING ITS SNARE, OFFER TO A KING?

*"Feathers, now growing, now falling out..."*
(A reference to Henry Fynn's bushy sideburns.)
*"Tamer of the evil-tempered elephant..."*
(Fynn's skill with firearms in hunting.)
*"Who was pregnant with many young ones..."*
(Fynn acquired several wives and fathered an unknown number of children during his time with the Zulu.)

Names of people and places were also often complex, themselves involving idiomatic descriptions. Two of the larger Zulu capitals during King Shaka's reign were KwaBulawayo and KwaDukuza, translated respectively (and somewhat ominously) as "The Place of Murder" and "The Place of Lost People."

King Shaka's own name has variations in the histories, depending on regional dialects. In the coastal lands south of the Thukela River, his name was pronounced "Tshaka." This would also explain why the early Port Natal settlers who were living in that area wrote "Chaka" in their written accounts, since that spelling indicates the "Tsh" sound. Those born upcountry in the lands of the Zulu usually spoke the king's name with the most commonly used pronunciation, "Shaka," which is the spelling we have chosen for this retelling of his legend.

The possible meanings of King Shaka's name reflect differing perceptions of the Zulu king. We cannot be certain of the true meaning – there are a number of versions of how he got his name, some less flattering than others. In Zulu territory there was a beetle known as "*itshaka*," which was believed to cause a bloated stomach symptomatic of intestinal distress. One story goes that, when Nandi became pregnant by Senzangakhona, she was said to be afflicted with this ailment, and King Shaka was given the name when he was born.

"*Itshaka*" also has another meaning, used to describe a girl who became pregnant out of wedlock, hence suggesting that King Shaka was illegitimate. This is quite possibly a convenient fabrication by later successors to vilify King Shaka and enhance their own reputations.

Another, somewhat more complimentary, version suggests that "Shaka" was not his birth name at all, but was actually bestowed later by King Dingiswayo, as part of the young warrior's praises: "*uSitshaka ka sitshayeki*" ("He who beats but is not beaten").

Whatever the truth may be, it is this last meaning that perhaps best reflects King Shaka's character.

# QUESTIONS AND IDEAS FOR GOING DEEPER

**The way in which the material in this book is organized uses the following pattern:**

- You start by reading (and viewing) the story just as it is.
- Next, there are questions and ideas to help you get a deeper understanding of what you have read.
- Finally, you think about how this applies to life as you know it (your own life, or the world in which you live).

You have read the story of King Shaka's reign and his murder. You have focused especially on the challenges he faced as a leader in a time of change. The questions that follow will require you to think what his story has to do with your life and the modern world you live in.

## CRITICAL THINKING QUESTIONS

**How accurate is this story ?**

- Some details in this storybook have been invented by the author. Does this mean that the story is not true?
- What is the difference between a fictional story and fake news?
- Is story telling important in your family? Why?

**The history of King Shaka's time**

- In what ways did the arrival of white settlers affect the Zulu people in King Shaka's time?
- How is your life affected by the history of colonial settlement?

**The challenges of leadership**

- King Shaka faced the dilemma of how to respond to the British settlers. What did he decide? What would you have done if you had been in his position?
- Think of a time when you had to make a difficult choice. Why was it difficult? How did you decide?

## Zulu political structures
- During the Festival of First Fruits, King Shaka spent a lot of his time doing political work. Why did he need to do this?
- Are modern leaders and celebrities able to have private lives?

## The role of women
- What effect did the key women in this story have on King Shaka's decisions?
- Why did King Shaka trust his sister's advice?
- In your community, do women have the same status as men? How do their roles differ? How do you feel about this?

## Zulu culture and beliefs
- The Zulu people in King Shaka's time believed their ancestors (*amadlozi*) could influence their lives for good or bad. Find examples in this story. What do you believe about the role of your ancestors?
- In Zulu culture it is unacceptable to speak the king's name without his title. Dingane repeatedly refers to "Shaka" instead of calling him "King Shaka." What does this show about his attitude to King Shaka?
- In this story, people consulted herbalists and sangomas who sought wisdom from the ancestors for their health needs. In modern society, who are the people trained to care for our health and spiritual well-being?

## Language and naming
- IsiZulu is a very expressive language. Look for examples of images that are used in this book.
- Imagery gives color to the language we use. Make a list of some images and idioms that we commonly use in English.
- How was your name chosen when you were born? Does it have a particular meaning?

# GLOSSARY

**Boer**
Dutch settler (literally, "farmer")

**Gogo**
grandmother

**ibutho** (plural: **amabutho**)
age-grade regiment

**idlozi** (plural: **amadlozi**)
ancestral spirits

**ikhanda** (plural: **amakhanda**)
royal military homestead

**imbongi** (plural: **izimbongi**)
praise singer

**imphepho**
aromatic plant used as incense,
burned during Zulu ceremonies

**inkosi** (plural: **amakhosi**)
chief/king

**inkosikazi** (plural: **amakhosikazi**)
female elder, part of the royal
house, or principal wife

**inyanga** (plural: **izinyanga**)
traditional healer

**isangoma** (plural: **izangoma**)
diviner, witchdoctor

**izibongo**
praises, chanted in honor of a king
or influential person

**isigodlo**
the royal enclosure at the upper
end of the *ikhanda*; also the women
of the king's household

**isiZulu**
the Zulu language

**iziYendane**
the name of one of Shaka's
regiments (*isiYendane* is literally a
person with a strange hairstyle)

**inkosi yami**
my chief/my king

**umKhosi**
The annual Zulu Ceremony of the
First Fruits

**umuthi** (plural: **imithi**)
traditional medicine; more
specifically occult medicine for
ritual purposes

# PRONUNCIATION

IsiZulu contains some sounds which are not used in English, but it uses letters from the English alphabet to represent them.

## CLICK SOUNDS: C, Q, AND X

**c**  To make the sound of the letter "c," suck the tip of the tongue against the palate, just behind your front teeth and then pull it away. This makes a soft click sound. It is like the sound English speakers use to show sympathy ("tsk.")

**q**  To make the sound of the letter "q," suck the tip of the tongue against the roof of your mouth, and then pull it away suddenly. This makes a hard click, like the sound English speakers use to imitate the sound of a horse's hoof on hard ground.

**x**  To make the sound of the letter "x," suck the side of the tongue against the inside of your cheek, and then pull it away suddenly. This is the sound that English speakers use to call a horse.

## ZULU PRONUNCIATION OF TH, PH AND KH

**th**  The English sound "th"(as in "thank" or "this") is not used in isiZulu. The letter combination "th" in isiZulu is sounded like the English letter "t." ("Sithole" sounds like "Sitole.")

**ph**  "ph" is pronounced like "p" and not like "f." (*Imphepho* sounds like "impepo.")

**kh**  "kh" is pronounced like "k" in "kick;" but "k" in isiZulu is pronounced more like "g," as in "gun." Thus "Shaka" sounds more like "Shaga."